Look for Omar's other adventures!

PLANET OMAR: Accidental Trouble Magnet

PLANET OMAR
UNEXPECTED SUPER SPY

ZANIB MIAN

ILLUSTRATED BY
NASAYA MAFARIDIK

G. P. PUTNAM'S SONS

G. P. PUTNAM'S SONS
An imprint of Penguin Random House LLC, New York

Text copyright © 2020 by Zanib Mian
Illustrations copyright © 2020 by Nasaya Mafaridik
Published by arrangement with Hodder and Stoughton Limited
First published in the United Kingdom in 2020
First American edition, 2020

Visit us online at penguinrandomhouse.com

Library of Congress Cataloging-in-Publication Data
Names: Mian, Zanib, author. | Mafaridik, Nasaya, illustrator.
Title: Unexpected super spy / Zanib Mian; illustrated by Nasaya Mafaridik.
Description: First American edition. | New York: G. P. Putnam's Sons, 2020. |
Series: Planet Omar; 2 | Summary: "Omar and his friends team up to raise money
to save his family's favorite mosque, and when the money goes missing,
they find the most unlikely culprit"—Provided by publisher.
Identifiers: LCCN 2020002520 (print) | LCCN 2020002521 (ebook) | ISBN 9780593109243 |
ISBN 9780593109250 (ebook)
Subjects: CYAC: Muslims—Fiction. | Fund raising—Fiction. | Humorous stories.
Classification: LCC PZ7.1.M514 Un 2020 (print) |
LCC PZ7.1.M514 (ebook) | DDC [Fic]—dc23
LC record available at https://lccn.loc.gov/2020002520
LC ebook record available at https://lccn.loc.gov/2020002521

Printed in the United States of America
ISBN 9780593109243
1 3 5 7 9 10 8 6 4 2

Design by Suki Boynton
Text set in Averia Serif Libre

This book is dedicated to all

the children who do something for someone else

just to put a smile on their face.

CHARLIE

my best friend

toothy grin extraordinaire

is SO double-jointed it's crazy!

has never tasted peanut butter, and would like to keep it that way

DANIEL

used to bully me and Charlie, but now we are friends

his sister, Suzy, has to go to the hospital a lot, which means he's on his best behavior at home

sometimes his worst behavior comes out at school

will surprise you with his hobbies

Mrs. ROGERS

CRR

CHAPTER 1

ASSSHHH!

That was the sound of my ceramic Stormtrooper bank breaking into 100 pieces. I had turned it upside down and tapped it against the metal leg of my desk, because I thought that was a good idea for getting the money out. It wasn't. But at least my money was there, and it looked like **A LOT.**

I needed to get it out to buy this really cool Nerf laser blaster I saw on TV. I had accidentally

broken my last one the time we had a Nerf battle at my cousin Reza's house. I'd been imagining that everyone was turning into MAN-EATING GIANTS WITH GREEN WARTS ALL OVER THEIR FACES and got a bit carried away. That's the best part—pretending you're running from something way scarier than your cousins and friends.

While I was counting my riches, Maryam came in and said, "YOU'RE SUCH AN IDIOT. You know there is a little rubbery piece at the bottom you can just open the thing with."

"I know," I said. I actually didn't know, so I felt kind of stupid. I tried really hard to think of something smart to say, but, in the

2

meantime, Maryam tried to sit on my wheelie chair, which wheeled itself away from her with a mind of its own. She completely missed the seat and hit the floor, and we both almost wet our pants laughing.

She disappeared back to her room after that, leaving me to add up all my coins and bills. In total, I had $42.53. Super cool—that had to be enough to buy the Nerf blaster! I borrowed

Mom's phone and called my best friend, Charlie.

After I told him, he said,

"WHOA! HOW DID YOU GET THAT MUCH?"

"I put all the money I got for Eid and all

the money I got for my birthday in there. Dad

said it would be worth the wait for something

awesome if I saved up."

"Aw, man, that's cool. I spend my money the

minute I get it."

I told Charlie that I used to do that, too, but

then I imagined that if I saved enough money,

one day I could pay people to let me drive even

though I'm only a kid. And maybe I would end

up with enough money to buy a Ferrari, because they're only like $150,000, which surely couldn't take that long to save.

Mom shouted up the stairs that it was time to get off the phone and put my shoes on to go to the mosque. But she said it really nicely and she even called me "sweetie," so I didn't think it was that urgent and I kept talking to Charlie and daydreaming about my Ferrari. Charlie was daydreaming, too, because I said I'd pay people to let him drive as well.

Then Mom came in and blew my ears off.

"I SAID PUT YOUR SHOES ON!"

Yikes!

"Bye, Charlie."

Our mosque trips had become even more fun since Dad started coming with us. He changed things around so that he doesn't have to go to the lab on Saturdays anymore, which means more cool things can happen on weekends now. He even took me go-karting recently, which was the **best Saturday ever!**

Gulp. I couldn't find my left shoe, and Mom was going to lose it if I didn't get this done

in fifteen milliseconds . . . Yes! I saw it
on top of the sofa and grabbed it while Dad
stood over me with a face like that emoji
whose lips are just a very straight line. But
when I went to put it on, I saw that it had
been treated to a dose of my little brother's

slime in a Bucket.

I didn't dare complain
or look for other shoes,
so I shoved my foot in. It
was DISGUSTING. Like I
was stepping on a

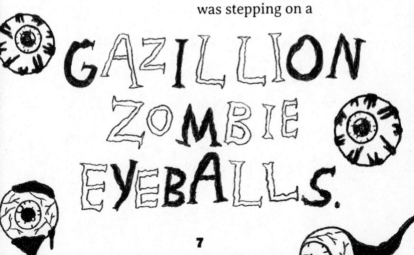

GAZILLION
ZOMBIE
EYEBALLS.

Ewwwwwhww.

I squished and SQUiRTEd my way to the Peanut (that's our car) and jumped in.

At the mosque, when we were all praying, Esa sat on my head and made me laugh. I had to control myself before it turned into a full-on giggle fit, so I imagined that there was a SUPER-VILLAIN holding me in a headlock and if I laughed out loud, he would blow up the whole entire universe. But if I kept quiet as a mouse, he would release me and the universe would be safe . . .

PHEW. I managed it. I was pretty pleased with myself, especially when Dad turned and winked at me when the prayer was finished. I know why he did it. To show me that he saw Esa on my head and that he was proud of how I'd handled it. Also because he was in a good mood. He's always in a good mood at the mosque, and he has a different sort of smile on his face while we're there. Maybe it's a *secret smile* that's only for Allah or something. I think he's really glad we found such a great mosque close to our new house. All the others Mom made us try out when we first moved are miles away. Dad says he's happy that it has the kind of vibes that make him feel closer to Allah. Mom and Dad like those kinds of vibes, and they say you don't get them in every mosque. Everyone is really nice to each other, and it's quiet, and light comes streaming in through the windows on sunshiny days.

CHAPTER 2

On Monday at school, I rolled in with an imaginary Nerf blaster in my arms and targeted my best friend, Charlie.

He gave me the very same toothy grin that made me like him when I moved to this school recently. Then he pulled out his own blaster from under the table (imaginary, too, of course) and pretended to blast me right back.

I think his imagination has been getting stronger since we became friends, like a muscle does when you lift weights all day long.

When Daniel saw us, he giggled and punched me on the arm. Don't worry, it was one of those FRIENDLY punches that don't hurt at all. Daniel is our friend now. He doesn't actually bully anyone anymore, not even Charlie, who used to be his favorite target for all things horrible. There's no way we'd be friends with a bully, but it turns out Daniel had reasons for being so naughty at school, and now that he has us as friends to hang out with, he's

TOTALLY DIFFERENT.

"It's a Nerf laser blaster," I announced. "Imaginary for now, but I'm going to get a real one with the money I've saved."

"Oh, cool!" said Daniel. "I want one."

"Me too!" chipped in Charlie.

"Let's all get them and have an

EPIC NERF BATTLE."

"We can all pretend to be spies, like James Bond chasing down an evil villain," Daniel said excitedly.

OH YEAAAAH!

Charlie and I said at the same time. We often say things at the same time, which is super funny and sometimes super freaky.

"Do you have enough money?" I asked.

"No, but my mom said she was going to

buy me something for, ummmm . . ." Daniel sheepishly scratched the back of his head instead of finishing his sentence.

"For what?"

Charlie and I did it AGAIN. Same words, same time. Same wanting to know what Daniel was getting a treat for.

"Umm . . ."

"For washing your dad's car?" I guessed.

"For cleaning your room?" Charlie guessed.

Daniel did some more sheepish head-scratching.

I tried another guess. "For getting ten out of ten on your spelling test?"

"No . . . no . . . um . . . actually for 'settling in so much better at school and making such good friends,'" Daniel said, using air quotes as he blushed bright red.

Charlie and I both jumped onto Daniel to give him a **hug**. I think he was blushing because he's not always 100% sure that we like him as our friend, but we super definitely do. We keep finding so many things that we like to do together—like the Nerf blasters!

We couldn't help but talk about it all during math, because it was way more exciting than learning about what a denominator was and how we could think about a pizza in fractions. The only thing I think when I see a pizza is how quick I can get it into my mouth. Mrs. Hutchinson was very excited about fractions. I could tell because her curly hair was all big and springy. That's one thing I like about Mrs. Hutchinson—she thinks everything is entertaining.

"I CANNOT WAIT for the Nerf battle. It's going to be crazy fun!" I whispered.

Charlie whispered back, "I knooowww. I just have to think of a way to convince my parents to buy me a blaster, too."

"You do know that both of you whisper as loud as you talk," Daniel pointed out.

He must have been right, because Mrs. Hutchinson came over, attempting to put her cross face on, and said, "Stop chatting and tell me how much pizza is on the board, boys."

"Not enough for me," said Daniel.

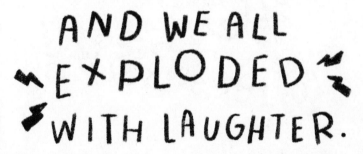

AND WE ALL EXPLODED WITH LAUGHTER.

HA HA HA HA HI HA HA

We had to clap our hands over our mouths quickly before Mrs. Hutchinson got upset.

Then Charlie said, "One-sixth," with his toothy grin.

HA HA HA HA

PHEW, Mrs. Hutchinson was pleased enough, even with all our giggling.

I couldn't wait to get home and ask Mom and Dad if they were OK with us having a big Nerf showdown at home and would they please order pizza that day. Maybe I could promise to talk about the pizza as fractions, like Mrs. Hutchinson was doing—then they'd be up for it for sure.

SO CHEESY!

They love brainy stuff like that. They say it's because they're scientists, but I think they're scientists *because* they like brainy stuff. It's like the chicken-and-egg situation.

CHAPTER 3

Mom picked me up on foot.

WHOA, did you just imagine her with a
SUPER-HUGE
FOOT, lifting me off the ground? I

did. But that's not what I meant. I meant that

she didn't bring her car. She walked. This is

her new thing. Walking as much as we can to

help the environment and be in good shape,

like Batman. It takes 13 minutes or 467 steps

to get home. I counted it the first time Mom

made us walk, and that number is *almost* correct. It would be more correct if Esa hadn't interrupted my counting by singing "Old MacDonald Had a Farm" at the top of his voice.

Today, instead of counting steps or imagining that if I stepped on a crack in the sidewalk it would cause an earthquake, like I sometimes do, I asked Mom about the Nerf battle.

"Please, Mom, you're so pretty."

I grinned.

"Funny!" said Mom. "You only tell me that when you want something . . ."

I laughed and switched on my pester-power puppy-dog eyes.

"OK, fine," she said. "As long you don't use tomato paste as monster guts like you did with Reza."

"I wouldn't dream of it!" I said. But my brain was bursting at the memory of how FUN that had been.

"And when did you say you wanted to do it?" She looked a bit sad now. "I don't think it can be this weekend, because we have to go to a meeting at the mosque on Sunday. They need to talk to us about raising enough money to keep it from closing down . . . It was just announced today on the WhatsApp group."

"**WHAAAAAT?**"

I said. "The mosque? Our mosque—

the secret-smile mosque?"

"Secret-smile mosque?" Mom said.

"Yeah! You and Dad have secret smiles in that mosque," I told her.

"Yes, then—the secret-smile mosque."

I couldn't believe it. My chest felt the way it did when our parakeet, Dodo, died when we lived in the old house.

"Wait. You said they have to raise money, right? So it might *not* have to close down?"

"That's right. Hopefully, it won't."

i dRAGGeD my feEt the rest of the way home.

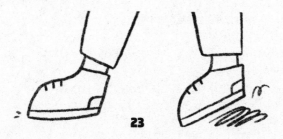

As soon as I got inside, **I SHOT UP THE STAIRS** to get my cash from its new hiding place. The best hiding place ever. It was rolled up in a green pair of underwear and placed carefully between my old shoes at the back of the closet. My underwear was something Maryam would never, EVER touch, no matter how desperate she was.

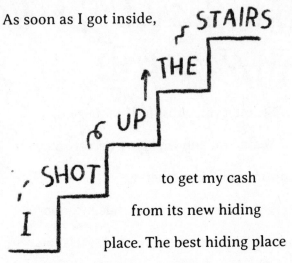

I took the $42.53 downstairs and put it on the table.

"That's for the mosque,"

I declared.

Mom got all melty-eyed. "But you were going to buy your Nerf blasty thingy with that money, sweetie."

"Nerf laser blaster, Mom. But it's OK. I want the mosque to have it. Now it won't have to shut down."

"Ummmmm, I think they need a bit *more* than that, stupid," said Maryam.

"Maryam!" Mom scolded. Then she came and took my chin in her hand and said, "That is so very wonderfully kind of you, Omar.

I am very, very proud of you right now.

I think the mosque does need a whole lot more, but we will find out on Sunday just how much."

Maryam scoffed, I guess because Mom wasn't proud of *her*.

"However much they need, I will get it!"

I said.

AND I MEANT iT.

I

SUPER

MEANT iT.

CHAPTER 4

That night, when I closed my eyes to go to sleep, I kept seeing a DINOSAUR, the size of an apartment building, destroying the secret-smile mosque with one flick of his tail and then picking up the little pieces and putting them on his ice cream, like they were sprinkles.

I didn't want to imagine that happening to the mosque. I shook my head and jumped out of bed. I had the fantastic idea of playing my Xbox to distract myself.

BUT FIRST, I HAD TO
SILENTLY 🚫 SNEAK 👣
DOWNSTAIRS IN THE DARK,
LIKE A BURGLAR 🕵. I
TIPTOED OUT OF MY ROOM,
AVOIDING THE SPOT" WHERE
THE SQUEAKY" FLOORBOARD
WAS. TO HELP ME
💣 CONCENTRATE, 💣 I
PRETENDED I WAS
STEPPING OVER
SECURITY LASERS
ON THE STAIRS THAT
WOULD SET OFF AN
ALARM~ IF I WASN'T
CAREFUL ENOUGH.

I made it! But just when I was about to buy a wicked new car in my game, Mom walked in and went wild.

"Omar! It's a school night! And what do I see? You're up at ten thirty. Ten thirty?! TEN! THIRTY! On your Playbox!"

I knew I was in TROUBLE, but I couldn't help giggling. "It's an Xbox, Mom. There's also such a thing as a PlayStation, which I wish I had as well . . . but, um, no Playbox."

DON'T BE SMART. INTO BED NOW, MISTER!

Dad poked his head around the door and said, "You have two seconds to shut that off and get into bed, smarty-pants."

"But it will take me at least seven seconds to walk upstairs to my bed."

"Right, that's it," said Dad, and he came and picked me up and held me under his arm like you would hold a soccer ball. Just like that. That's because he's big and really strong.

We both giggled as he plunked me down onto my bed. Dad put his finger to his lips and nodded toward little snoring Esa. "Shh now, and get some sleep," he whispered.

This time when I closed my eyes, I saw

Dad's Secret Smile.

I couldn't bear the thought of him losing it. I had to dream up a clever way to raise more money . . .

CHAPTER 5

The next day at school, I waited till lunchtime
to tell Daniel and Charlie that I was really
sorry but I wouldn't be able to buy a Nerf
blaster for myself after all, which meant we
couldn't have an epic Nerf battle.

I didn't want to tell them in the morning,
because Mrs. Hutchinson had started the day
with an awesome cookie-decorating session
for us. She had brought in all sorts of toppers
and sprinkles and bits of fudge and
M&M's. And, as you know, that isn't

something that teachers
do very often. She said
it was a lesson about "how to
prepare food," but I'm pretty sure
it was mostly because she likes
chocolate chips and she likes us—
that's another reason why she's

the BEST
TEACHER ever!

Charlie and Daniel were so happy,
gobbling candy and piling all the
available toppings onto cookies,
that I just kept my mouth shut
about the bad news.

At lunchtime, we got SMELLY
cauliflower spring rolls with steamed

"carrots," which may as well have been steamed sloth fingers, because they were so brown and gross. After we had finished complaining about the school cook and wondering how much it would cost to get a real chef at our school, I blurted out the bad news. "I have to tell you something . . . I can't buy a Nerf blaster anymore."

Daniel jumped up as if his bottom had been

PRICKED BY A HEDGEHG

and ran in circles around Charlie and me, screaming,

"NOOOOOOO!"

Charlie looked at me with a smile so big I could almost see his gums. He liked it when Daniel behaved all wild, as long as it wasn't against him or us, like it used to be.

"Because, Daniel . . ." I said loudly over his screaming, "the mosque is going to close down if they don't get enough money."

Daniel stopped suddenly with his jaw dropped and said, "Really?"

"Yes. Super really."

He started up again, and this time Charlie and I joined in.

When our lungs screamed back at us to stop, we fell onto the floor.

I had known Daniel would
be upset, too. Ever since we
got lost together on the London
Underground and were chased by a not-really-
zombie, Daniel has often talked about the
London Central Mosque—because that's where
we ended up being rescued. I think he's decided
that mosques have superpowers or something.
He even insisted on going to my local mosque
with me once to see what it was like and
whether they have halal candy there, too.

(They do. Daniel ate three and went home with a blue tongue.)

We made a new friend there that day, a girl named Aisha who doesn't go to our school but who likes Batman almost as much as Daniel does. That kind of nice thing often happens at the mosque, not just for kids but for grown-ups, too. That's probably another reason why Dad has a secret smile there—he says that it isn't just a place for praying; it's a place where a single person becomes part of something bigger. I'm not exactly sure what he means by that, but I guess the mosque IS quite a lot

BIGGER

than a house. You couldn't fit everyone who goes there into our living room for tea and snacks . . . though I bet my mom would try it if she could.

After we'd fallen down on the floor, we were all quiet for a little while. Then Daniel whispered, "No," in a very small voice.

"No," whispered Charlie.

"No," I whispered, too.

And we decided right there that we were all going to help the mosque together.

CHAPTER 6

It was the first Sunday in three months that we

had to cancel our family tradition of

SCIENCE SUNDAYS,

because the meeting in the mosque was in the

morning, and Science Sunday always happens

in the morning. Everything at our house has its

set time and day and exactness, as if life is

ONE BIG SCiENcE

eXPERiMENT.

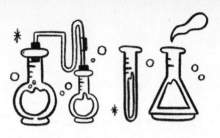

Morning is Mom and Dad's favorite time. They always wake up early, even over the holidays, and act as if they've drunk loads of soda, even before breakfast. Some days, Dad takes his motorcycle out after his dawn prayers so he can enjoy the empty roads. Mom always worries that he goes too fast. He always says, "Don't worry, darling. I'm safe with it." But I know he's not, because I've seen his face when he drives the Peanut and gets to go fast on the highway. He looks like a kid who's just been given a lifetime supply of Oreos. (By the way, I've *always* wanted a lifetime supply of Oreos.

I love them, and I know seventeen different ways to eat them. If Mom hadn't refused to buy them for me anymore, I would know at least thirty-seven by now . . .)

Anyway, back to Sunday. I couldn't wait to start planning MØN£¥making 1ĐEa$. Charlie and Daniel were going to come over when we got back from the mosque so we could start.

At the meeting we found out that they needed to raise $30,000. The imam of the mosque spoke to everybody. He looked like he was sad but trying not to be.

"We've discovered an urgent issue with the mosque building.

It's holding for now, but it's something we need to get working on in a few weeks. The woodwork in the roof is rotting."

The whole roomful of people looked nervously up at the ceiling.

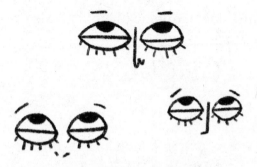

"Now, unfortunately, we don't have enough funds to pay for the work needed to fix everything, and if we can't raise it, we will have to close the mosque because it won't be safe," the imam finished.

PHEW, I thought. That sounds kind of easy. I think I could raise $30,000 with my friends. And other people would be raising money with their family and friends, too, so I was sure it would be OK. But the best bit was that the imam said that if you're involved with making a mosque, or you stop one from shutting down, Allah will build a house for you in *Paradise.*

whoa. whoa. WHOA!

I couldn't believe it. I imagined Allah making a house for ME. And because He's God, He would know *exactly* what I want in my dream house: it would have one room made

entirely of **trampolines**,
even the walls! One room would
be a **theater**, with reclining
seats, so tons of friends could come.
There would be **popcorn machines**
in there, too. There would super

definitely be a game room, with
all my favorite video games,
and I think if I was in
heaven, I would even be
allowed to play the games that Mom
and Dad have forbidden me to play on
Earth. The kitchen would be built entirely of
oreos, and the only other things
available to eat and drink in there would be
PIZZA and **milkshakes**. You could
break the Oreos off the wall if you wanted,

and they would just grow back. In the bedroom, the whole floor would be a waterbed, so you could just drop and sleep wherever you wanted.

And there would be no roof, so you could see the stars and planets in the sky. Anything that you threw on the floor would magically put itself away in the closet or on the shelves. Oh, and all my favorite authors would be there, all ready to read me a story. And of course Mom and Dad, because they're the best at telling stories. (Don't tell my friends, but I still really love it when someone reads me a story.) I guess Maryam and Esa could be there, too.

I was so busy imagining my *dream house* that I didn't realize it was time to leave the mosque until Maryam flicked my ear.

"What the TOAD SKIN was that for?"

"For being such a daydreaming piece of ostrich gut!"

In case you're wondering about this strange way of insulting each other, it all began when Mom was driving and a bus pulled out when it shouldn't have, almost causing an accident, and Mom shouted,

"WHAT THE BUS ?!!"

Maryam and I had looked at each other and raised our eyebrows all the way to the tops of our foreheads, because we saw what Mom did there. She swore . . . without swearing . . .

And then a couple of days later, Mom dropped a butternut squash onto her toes and screamed,

"SHHHHHH-UGAR AND TWO PANCAKES!"

That was so random that Maryam and I rolled all over the floor laughing, and we repeated it to each other and cracked up again and again. Ever since then, we've been trying to come up with more and more inventive insults. (I think I'm winning.)

HA HA HA HA

As we drove home, I was feeling excited. Not only was I going to help save the mosque with my friends, but I was going to get my dream house for doing it!

CHAPTER 7

I ran to the door when Charlie and Daniel arrived.

Daniel was sporting a red nose, because he had a cold. Dad looked horrified. He's super scared of germs, because when he gets sick, he gets really sick. He says it's a

SCIENTIFIC FACT

that man flu is worse than the flu that kids and women get,

but Mom says it's only because we're a lot tougher than he is.

My friends and I went straight up to my bedroom, and I shoved Esa's toys under his bed to make space.

"Let's brainstorm," I said. "Mrs. Hutchinson always makes us do that to think of ideas."

"OK," said Charlie.

Daniel blew his nose and nodded his head.

So I got a piece of paper and my Sharpies and wrote:

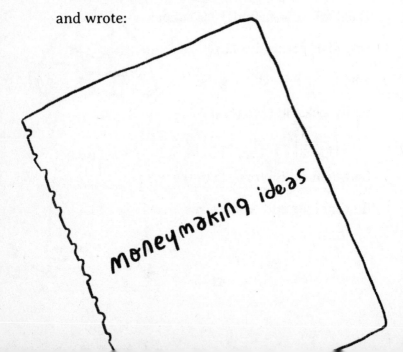

moneymaking ideas

"Right, guys. Shoot," I said.

"'Lemonade' stand," said Daniel.

"Lemonade?" I said.

"Yeah."

I wrote it down.

"My uncle sells things on eBay,"

Charlie said.

"Like what?"

"Like earphones and fans and stuff like that."

"Cool. But where can we get those from?"

I said.

"We beed bongey," said Daniel.

Charlie and I must have looked confused,

because he tried again. "You bow—we dob't

have aby. We're brying to *babe* bongey."

"We do have $42.53," I said, figuring out his blocked-nose secret code. "I wonder how many earphones we can buy with that."

"Or we can just *make* stuff to sell," said Charlie.

I wrote that down.

Then I told them my idea. "Let's hold a talent contest and charge people money to come and see it! It would be so great!"

"Cool!" said Charlie and Daniel both at the same time.

"How much should we charge, and where will we have it? Maybe I could ask my parents if we can have it here in the backyard or something . . ."

"Or maybe at the mosque?" said Charlie.

"Oh yeah. Good idea. They have a huge room."

I wrote down **tALЄhT· CONteST**, and we kept thinking.

"Do chores for bongey," Daniel suggested.

"Like cleaning our rooms," said Charlie with a cheeky grin.

We all

CRACKED UP laughing

at the thought of asking our parents for money for cleaning our rooms.

Daniel laughed too hard before he managed to grab a tissue and got snot all down his face.

"Ewwwwwww, Daniel!"

I couldn't breathe anymore from laughing. Ouch, ouch—it hurt!

There's something about snot that is funny and disgusting at the same time. Like farts.

(Especially when Maryam farts after we've had curry and she pretends it isn't her...)

Anyway, by the time we were done, we had lots of ideas to get started on:

everyone bring
something
to school
on monday
↑
make stuff
to sell

when ?
↑ where ?
↑
talent
contest

moneymaking ideas

do
cleaning ← chores → washing
bedroom   car
↓   ↓
walking   weeding
people's   garden
dogs

I was starving after all that thinking! Or maybe it was more because Mom has been making these funny  healthy muffin things for breakfast. They are

SUPER YUCK and SUPER DRY.

Dad pretends that he likes them so that he doesn't hurt Mom's feelings, but once I caught him smothering one with peanut butter when Mom wasn't looking. Before we went to the mosque, I had put mine in the pocket of my bathrobe and just pretended I'd eaten it.

Have you ever been so hungry you felt like you had a huge hole in your chest? I don't understand it, because it should be my tummy that has a problem with being hungry, but for some reason it feels more like my chest needs food to fill it up. Sometimes it feels like the hole is so big it could be a GAPING WORMHOLE, ready to suck in anything I walk past! I imagined Charlie jumping into it and ending up in some other dimension. I wondered whether he would find me and Daniel in that other dimension and what we would look like there . . . Probably completely different, with green hair or something.

Luckily, Dad had made his famous spaghetti Bolognese as a treat, since my friends were staying to eat lunch with us. He puts stuff in it that he won't tell us about, but I don't mind, because it makes it taste deeelicious. I'm OK . . . as long as he's not adding

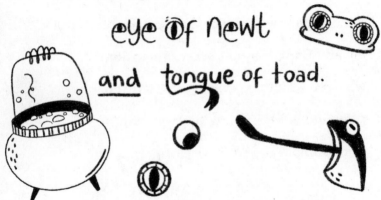

eye of newt and tongue of toad.

I guess it wasn't just me who was super hungry, because Charlie, Daniel, Maryam and even Esa shoved down the Bolognese without saying a word from start to finish. When I had eaten every last bite, I looked up and realized

I was the only one who got it all over my shirt.

I'm such a *messy eater* that Mom doesn't let me order spaghetti if we go out to eat. Also, it's not usually halal at restaurants.

As soon as Daniel's and Charlie's parents had picked them up, Mom said, "Right, who wants to do the grocery shopping with me?"

PING! A CHORE!

Perfect opportunity, I thought, and volunteered myself super quick.

"I'll do it with you, and I'll pack the bags and unpack them back at home. All for $2.50!"

"Don't be so cheeky!" said Dad. "Since when do you get paid to help out?"

I shrugged. "It's part of the plan to raise money for the mosque."

That made Dad change his mind pretty fast. He said he was really proud of me and my friends for being such stars. And then he said of course I could have $2.50 for helping with the shopping. In fact, I could have $5.00.

YESSSSS!

Maryam said, "Humph. That's so unfair," and she stormed off to get her coat.

I like doing the grocery shopping with my parents, because I can get stuff that they wouldn't normally buy when they go on their own. Sometimes I ask them if I can pretty please have this or that, but sometimes I just sneak it into the packed cart.

Esa is too big now to sit in the cart like he used to, so I also have to put up with him following me and picking stuff up. Once, he even dropped a jar of pasta sauce on the floor and **smashed it to smithereens**, which was **sooooooooooo embarrassing.**

I wasn't sure if I should run away and pretend

I didn't know him, or stick around and help

Mom deal with it.

This time, he started flinging sausages into the cart at the speed of Dad's motorcycle.

"What are you doing, chipmunk?" said Mom. "You can't have all those; they're not halal."

Esa is still learning all about the food he can't eat when he's at preschool or restaurants and things, because of being Muslim and needing to **EAT ONLY HALAL FOOD,** حلال

which has been prepared in a special way. It can be confusing for little kids, since chicken is OK at home, because we get the halal kind. But at school, it's not halal, and Esa doesn't always understand.

Maryam teases him for being such a **dummy,** but I feel a little sorry for him, because he gets sad when he can't eat things he's chosen. Like after the sausages, he chose some *Candy* that had gelatin in them, so he got told they weren't halal and he almost burst into tears. I helped him find some halal ones that said they were vegan and got a pack for myself, too . . . Well, I deserved them for working so hard on this chore.

CHAPTER 8

At school on Monday, we huddled together to share what we had brought in to sell to kids on the playground. Charlie had made yummy cookies at home with his mom, and Daniel had made . . . wait for it . . .

WHAAAAAT!
DANIEL CAN
DO ORIGAMI??

Charlie and I couldn't believe it! We
couldn't stop quizzing him about whether he
was kidding. Did his dad make them? Did he
buy them? No. Apparently, he'd been folding
paper into things since he was six, but he'd
just never shown anyone before. After that,
the hard candy that I had found in my bedside

table and shoved in my bag to sell didn't seem so great. We walked around the playground, shyly approaching kids, asking them to buy our things. Some kids just laughed and ran away. LOTS of kids told Daniel that he DID NOT make those birds, and Charlie and I told them they could bet their best friends' teeth that he did.

Sarah from our class really cheekily said,

Can I have a cookie for free?

"No," said Daniel. "It's 50 cents and no less, because it's delicious."

"Charlie would give me one for free, because he's *kind*!" teased Sarah, with one hand on her hip.

Charlie blushed bright red and immediately handed over a free cookie. Daniel and I said in unison,

"GEEEEZ, CHARLIE!"

After a while of walking around, we finally realized something: DUHHHHH, kids don't usually bring money to school with them.

"What will we do? If we can't sell stuff to kids at school, who will we sell it to?" said Daniel.

"Maybe we can ask Mrs. Hutchinson if she can talk to the parents and tell them to give their kids some money," I suggested.

"Do you think she would listen to us?" said Daniel, who had seen the angry side of Mrs. Hutchinson a lot when he was more of a troublemaker.

"Definitely. She's really cool. She always helps," Charlie assured him.

"You ask her, Charlie," I said, because no matter how nice she was, I still felt too shy to ask her something like that.

"Why me?" pleaded Charlie.

"'Cause you have the best smile," I said, quickly thinking of one reason we all like him so much.

Charlie went red again and said that we should all ask her together.

"It's a plan," said Daniel.

"Yup," I agreed.

So we went to find Mrs. Hutchinson, who looked like she had just started her lunch, even though it was nearly the end of lunchtime. Her hair told me why: she had been very busy. Her hair couldn't hide anything. It was all over the place. Some curls looked like they had to be somewhere else, while others were desperately trying to eat her lunch.

We told her all about the plan to raise money so that the mosque wouldn't have to close down. She looked at us as if she was about to

BURST WITH PRIDE

and love or something. I wondered: If a human ever did actually burst with pride and love, would balloons and confetti and cotton candy come flying out of them?

"You are such generous children!" she said. "I'm going to help you as much as I can, but the thing is that I can't speak to parents without Mr. McLeary approving it. He *is* the principal. I'll arrange a meeting for the three of you to tell him about your idea."

Gulp!

Mr. McLeary is the meanest meanie in the school. Everyone calls him MR. McSCARY behind his back. I have literally NEVER seen him smiling at a kid.

And now we were at his mercy . . .

CHAPTER 9

As soon as I got home from school and downed a bag of chips (and the apple that Mom said I had to have if I wanted the chips), I went over to see my next-door neighbor, Mrs. Rogers.

"Now, there's a lovely face I haven't seen in a while," she said when she opened her door.

"I've been busy making plans to save the mosque!" I told her.

"Save the mosque? Well, that sounds heroic. What are you saving it from?"

"FROM MAN-EATING ZOMBIES!"

"Oh no, when are they coming? I'll put it in my calendar," said Mrs. Rogers.

Hahahaha!

She is always unexpectedly hilarious. She surprises me every time I see her, and I am not an easy kid to surprise, because my imagination has already thought of everything. It's so much better now than when we first moved in and she didn't like us.

After we finished giggling, I told her about the real situation.

"So, I actually came over to ask you if I can do some chores for you and get paid," I said, smiling my best smile.

"Sure. You can start by washing my car."

Mrs. Rogers's car was one of the surprising things about her. My nani doesn't drive, and I've never seen any other people *that old* driving, but Mrs. Rogers still drives her car all the time.

She looked at me as if she was reading my thoughts, which I'd kept to myself because Mom and Dad say it's not polite to call people old.

"I'm as sharp as a bat, you know," she said. "Don't be fooled by this wrinkly skin."

And she winked.

She handed me $8 and I did the best I could, which must have been not too bad because Mrs. Rogers seemed pleased once I was done. I had imagined **teeny-tiny STORMTROOPERS** helping me, which made it way better, especially when my fingers were cold. Why were they teeny-tiny? Because normal-size Stormtroopers would just be normal and that's only half as fun.

Back at home, Mom was exhausted.

"I can't wait to get off my feet!" she kept saying as she stirred the lamb korma we were having for dinner.

Hmmm, I thought. I knew how I could make her feel better and earn some money at the same time. She did everything for us all day long. She deserved a

SPA Treatment.

So while she finished cooking, I went upstairs to get things ready.

I thought for the very best spa experience, I'd have to stimulate all five senses. I got some of Mom's lotions and face creams out and put them on her bedside table. Then I went downstairs to get some cucumber. I saw a cardboard box from a package Mom had opened earlier with those soft white things in it for protection. Perfect. I grabbed that.

Next, I went into Maryam's room for one of her Lindor chocolates, which I know she keeps hidden in her bedside table.

She screamed at me, of course.

"Sorry." I grinned like I was the yellow emoji with all the teeth showing.

 "It's just that I'm trying to make Mom feel relaxed, and a chocolate treat is part of it . . . so I was wondering if I can have one of yours to give her?"

To my HUGE SURPRISE, she softened up right away and threw one at me with a smile.

"Thanks!" I said.

Teenagers are super weird.

Next, I made a sign and stuck it up in the hallway.

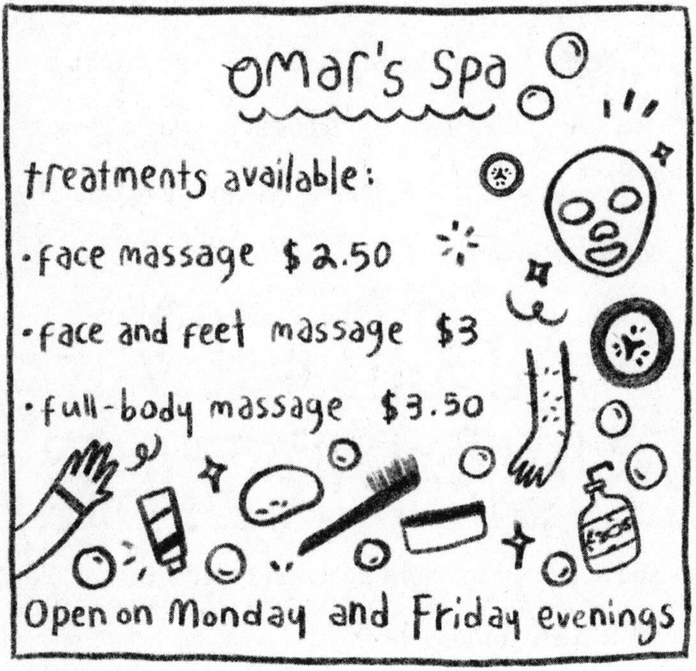

Omar's Spa

treatments available:

- face massage $2.50
- face and feet massage $3
- full-body massage $3.50

Open on Monday and Friday evenings

Well, I couldn't be stuck rubbing people's feet every day. I still wanted to play with my stuff sometimes.

"Mom! Come to my spa."

"Your spa???"

"Yes, come, come. Quickly!"

Mom came upstairs, although she was very confused. I made her lie down on her bed and quickly plonked the cucumber slices on her eyes. I had seen that somewhere on TV.

"*Eek!*" Mom squealed, reaching for the cucumbers. "What is that?"

"It's cucumber, Mom. Just be still and keep those on your eyes. I'm going to relax your tired feet now." I put the box of white things on the bed and stuck both her feet into it.

Mom giggled a bit.

Next, I got a dollop of cream and started rubbing it on her face.

"Um, wow . . ." said Mom. But she sounded like it wasn't *wow*, so I had to step things up.

"Open your mouth."

"Ummmm, OK. What are you going to put in it?" she asked. She sounded scared.

"Just open it! And keep your eyes closed. I'm stimulating all your five senses."

I shoved the chocolate through her hesitating lips.

She relaxed a little bit, I could tell. She likes Lindor.

Then I remembered I hadn't stimulated the

hearing sense. I cranked the
volume up and hit PLAY on my
iPad. It was "Sunflower" from
the *Spider-Verse* movie.

Mom

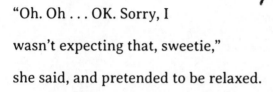

jumped.

"Oh. Oh . . . OK. Sorry, I
wasn't expecting that, sweetie,"
she said, and pretended to be relaxed.

"I'm going to massage your feet now," I
announced.

I tipped out some lotion. Lots of it.

"Oh, that's cold," said Mom. But then after a
while, she added, "It does feel good, actually. I
needed that."

FINALLY, I thought.

Oops, I forgot the fifth sense. Smell. I ran to the bathroom and got the air freshener. I thought seven quick squirts should do the job.

Mom coughed a bit and choked out, "Ummm, can I go downstairs? I need to check the curry."

"No, you have to stay like that for two hours," I explained. Well, nobody can relax properly in ten minutes. "Dad's home now. I'll ask him to check it."

Mom said, "Ooooookay . . ." and gave in.

She didn't end up staying two hours in the end, because we had to have dinner. I was glad

anyway; I didn't realize how slow two hours
can be when you're rubbing someone's feet.
Mom gave me $10 instead of the $3
I had written on the sign for the spa.
As soon as the bill hit my hand,
Maryam appeared from nowhere with
a scowl on her face.

"Dinosaur's fart," she said.
She was referring to me. "You think you're
clever, but last night I saw you trying to open
a wall to get into the bathroom."

"Yeah, right!" I said. This was such a
hilarious thought. I chuckled super loud.

But Maryam wasn't chuckling with me.
She was looking at me as if she
was a rhino and I was getting
in the way of its water hole.

GULP. I knew that face. She was up to something.

CHAPTER 10

Have you ever had wobbly knees?

I mean actual, literal wobbly knees. I could feel
mine shaking as I stood in line with the rest
of the class waiting to go into the classroom
on Tuesday morning. It was supposed to be
a straight line, and it sort of was, except half
the kids were doing this new dance from
a computer game we all like. Even Daniel!
Anyway, back to my knees. They were wobbly
because it was the day we had to speak to

MR. MCSCARY about selling stuff to the other kids. Charlie had arrived with his glasses on all wonky, as if they were wobbly just like my knees.

We hated to remind Daniel what day it was, but we had to. As soon as we told him, Daniel stopped waving his arms around and we all stood there not talking at all.

To make things worse, we had to get through half the day first, because Mr. McScary was going to meet us at lunchtime. Luckily, we had some fun lessons, like science and making up rhyming poems in language arts. Here's mine:

Food is cool, food is nice.
Sometimes it is full of spice.
I like the color and the taste.
I won't let it go to waste.
But there are some things I'll never eat.
Like the eye of a newt or dragon's feet.

It's not my best poem, but at least it rhymes!

When we ate our lunch, my sandwich was having extra trouble traveling down my throat. I imagined myself as one of those **skinny snakes** that can eat a whole egg without chewing it, and it goes down really awkwardly and slowly.

Daniel wolfed down his lunch in less than a minute. I guess that's how he eats when he's nervous. And then there was Charlie. He smiled and nodded the whole time he was eating, as if he was reminding us and himself that it was going to be OK.

We went to meet Mrs. Hutchinson after

we'd eaten, and she walked us over to Mr. McLeary's office.

"Will you stay with us?" I asked.

"Yes, I'll stay with you," said Mrs. Hutchinson, winking. Her heels were making

click -clack

noises and her hair was bouncing to the rhythm. It made me sort of want to pull one of her curls to see what it would do. So I shoved my hands in my pockets.

When we knocked, Mr. McLeary said, "Uh . . . come in, we've just finished here."

He was brushing crumbs off his sweater, but they just landed on his pants, which were black, so I could see at least seven crumbs. He must have been eating his lunch at the same time as doing a principal punishing routine, because a grumpy-looking kid from third grade was being marched out of the office by her teacher.

This seemed to turn Daniel's feet into

BLOCKS
OF CEMENT

that he couldn't move forward anymore.

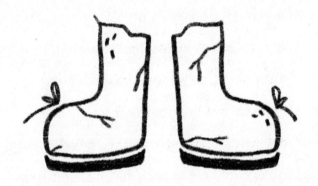

"Maybe I shouldn't come in . . ." he whispered.

I guess he was thinking of all the times he'd been sent in there as the naughty kid. "It'll be fine," I said, and gave his hand a squeeze. The squeeze seemed to melt his cement blocks, because we all ended up in chairs in front of Mr. McScary's desk.

Mrs. Hutchinson began to explain the whole fundraising project, while our hearts thudded in our chests. I could hear Daniel's and Charlie's . . . or was that just mine? I grabbed Charlie's hand under the table and squeezed it, too. Charlie squeezed mine back. Mr. McScary's lips were pulled in and pressed together really hard, as if he was trying to hide them. The only word he'd said so far was "uh-huh."

Then I could hear Mrs. Hutchinson saying, "Go on, Omar, tell Mr. McLeary what kind of things you want to sell."

My words were stuck in my head. I tried to imagine my old pal H_2O. He's the

cool steam-breathing dragon

I used to imagine all the time when I needed more confidence. Things had been going so well lately that H_2O hadn't made an appearance for a while. But I needed him now, so I quickly thought of him swooping down with a big dragon grin! He was holding cookies and origami birds in his hands, and then he started juggling them.

I don't know how long I sat without speaking, but when Mrs. Hutchinson said, "Omar?" I was ready.

"Mr. McLeary, thank you for listening to our ideas. We would like to sell delicious homemade cookies, origami birds made by my friend Daniel here, and maybe our old toys and books. It's probably best to set up a table to sell them at lunchtime or after school."

Charlie and Daniel were staring at me as if they were thinking

WHOA, you Said it!

I was impressed by my own grown-up-ness.

Then Charlie sat up straight and said, "*Organic* cookies!" with a big Charlie kind of smile.

Mr. McLeary cleared his throat. *Here it comes*, I thought. *He's going to say something like*

ABSOLUTELY NOT, YOUNG MAN.

But then I got a huge surprise.

"Yes. Sure. Of course you can. I'm impressed. Great initiative, all of you. Well done."

And then the weirdest thing happened . . . Mr. McLeary's lips curled up into a

He was smiling at us? Amazing!

I thought of H_2O's juggling, and I realized what he was trying to tell me. Encouraged by the not-so-scary principal's smile, I blurted out,

Everyone looked at me.

"We're planning a talent contest to raise money, but we need a stage. What do you think about us having it in the school auditorium, Mr. McLeary? We could even sell the things on the same day instead of at lunchtime."

Mrs. Hutchinson's curls perked up.

Charlie and Daniel were nodding their heads in agreement.

"Sure, why not?" said Mr. McLeary. "That's really good thinking. I'll make arrangements."

And he smiled again.

We filed out of his office and spent the rest of the day bouncing around with excitement, which was perfect for after-school soccer club. Daniel scored six goals.

OH, YEAAAH!

Six goals was two more than Jayden, who is used to being the best scorer. But Jayden was a good sport, because he still high-fived Daniel at the end, and Ellie gave him one of the key rings that hung on her bag. (She still had sixteen of them left.)

When Mom picked me up, I didn't shut up about everything all the way home, and as soon as I got inside, I ran upstairs to tell Maryam the great news.

But when I bounced into her room, she wasn't alone. She had her friends over.

"OH MY GOD. OMAR. YOU CAN'T JUST BARGE INTO MY ROOM WHENEVER YOU LIKE!"

They were plotting ways to raise funds for the mosque. I looked at the ideas they had written down, and in bold across the top it said:

Objective:
Make more money than Omar and his friends.

CHAPTER 11

I called Charlie, and then Daniel, right away. We couldn't believe Maryam's sneaky plot!

"She's such a GIANT SNAKE-EATING LIZARD," I said.

"Yeah, she's a HAIRY TOAD," said Daniel.

"Charlie said she was an ELEPHANT WITH ITS BOTTOM ON ITS FACE." I giggled.

And then we laughed so hard at our alternative swear words that we forgot all about how annoying Maryam was.

I guess it wasn't too bad anyway, because it meant more money for the mosque, but I still didn't want to lose. I wanted us to make way more money than Maryam and her friends ever could! After all, she was doing it for silly and mean reasons, and we were actually doing it to save the mosque. Mom and Dad always say that the reason why you're doing something is super important, because you could be doing something good for the wrong reasons, like just getting people to say that you're **awesome**. But even if you're doing something that you think isn't that fantastic but it's for a great reason, then that's better. I thought about that, and decided that Allah would be on our side. Though then I wondered if He would approve of taking sides . . . Well, if He did,

He'd be on ours for sure!

TEAM OMAR

We knew we had to work really hard to make sure Maryam's friends wouldn't win. We spent every lunchtime and every recess during the whole week planning our talent contest and the things we'd sell. Mrs. Hutchinson was helping us a lot. We chose her to be on the panel of judges, along with Mr. McLeary and the three of us. She said that she'd see which of the school board members wanted to be on the panel, too.

That Thursday, when we got the date from Mr. McLeary for when we could use the auditorium, Mrs. Hutchinson spoke to the whole school about it so that kids would know and could start to plan what their talent would be. Then she made Charlie, Daniel and me stand up, because we were the organizers.

"Sheesh," Daniel whispered,

"I feel so IMPORTANT."

We all did. Especially because now that everyone knew, kids kept coming up to us on the playground to tell us, or even show us, what their talents were. Like there was this second-grade kid who knew Dr. Seuss's *Green Eggs and Ham* by heart, and he literally went through it without blinking. And there was this other kid in fourth grade who could do a

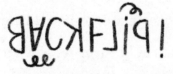

"Are we allowed to enter, too?" asked Charlie.

"Hmmm, good question," I said. "I guess we could, but we ARE judges, so maybe it wouldn't be fair . . ."

"What if me and Charlie entered and you were a judge, Omar?" said Daniel.

"Sure," I said.

"Thank you, thank you, Sam-I-Am," said Charlie with a grin. "I'm going to do something with my double joints!"

"I'm going to sing!" said Daniel.

"WHAAAAAT?"

I'm not sure that Charlie and I are ever going to run out of surprises when it comes to Daniel.

I wondered what my talent could be. Once, my mom told me that my smile was so real and happy that I could make anyone do anything with it. I imagined performing this talent at the contest, hYpNⓄti'zⒾNg the whole crowd with my smile and then making everyone do wacky things, like pat their heads and rub their tummies at the same time while sticking their tongues out. It would be so funny. And then I decided that if it worked on Mr. McLeary, I would super definitely get him to change the school lunch to

PiZZA and FRiES

every day (except Fridays, when it would be fish 'n' chips!).

The best part was designing the tickets.

Mrs. Hutchinson said that we could draw them and then the school would print them out and sell them to parents at the end of the day.

Here's what we came up with (I drew the kid juggling):

An evening of entertainment.
Come and watch our talent contest!

Prize: YOUR PICK—
an Oxford dictionary
OR
a gumball machine!

Just $2 to enter the contest.
Tickets: $3
Auditorium, Tuesday, 7pm

OK, the prizes weren't great, but we didn't really have money to buy better ones and Mr. McLeary kindly offered those. We were pretty sure NOBODY would pick the dictionary, but we didn't feel like we could say that to Mr. McLeary.

I couldn't wait for the weekend, when Charlie and Daniel would be coming over to make lots of stuff to sell on the day. But, as you might have guessed,

Miserable Madam Maryam almost ruined it all ...

CHAPTER 12

I know it's good to be **ambitious**.
Mom and Dad are always talking about it. But
Maryam and her friends took the ambitious
thing and went *loopy* with it.

On Saturday morning, when I was lost in
my Xbox games, waiting for *my* friends to
come over, Maryam had invited *her* group,
too. I only found out when Daniel and Charlie
rang the doorbell. Maryam's
friends were taking up the
entire kitchen table with their

paint mess. (Mom only lets us paint in the kitchen, where there's no carpet.) You won't believe this, but they were trying to paint pictures that they could sell for $500 each. They were doing it even though (or maybe because) Mrs. Rogers's son, John, is an artist and he says it's hard to sell art, but when you do, you can make a lot of money.

In fact, Mrs. Rogers was sitting with them, telling them to make another splatter here and darken the tones there.

She looked up at me with a sly grin that I didn't even know grandmas could have. That face told me she knew Maryam couldn't sell any of those paintings for that much money, and it was hilarious.

"DAAAAAAAAAD!"

I complained.
"Where are my
friends and I going to make
our stuff? We need the kitchen
table, too!"

"You can do yours tomorrow,
brat face," said Maryam.
Her friends giggled.
My friends grimaced.

"Tomorrow is Science Sunday, missy," snapped Mom.

Esa picked up a paintbrush and started
painting his own face, while Dad tried to figure
out what to do.

Then Mrs. Rogers said, "You can use my kitchen."

"Really?" said Dad. "That won't be a problem? We don't want to be a bother."

Seriously cheesy . . . My dad was too polite sometimes.

"We'll take it!" I said quickly, before Mrs. Rogers changed her mind.

So Mrs. Rogers and her kitchen were all ours for the day, which was super excellent because when we baked the cookies, she let us use her

mother's secret recipe.

"Mrs. Rogers is old, so if this recipe is her mom's, that means it's from the olden days," Daniel whispered as we sampled the first batch.

Oh, Delicious Mother of all Cookies!

We stopped and stared at each other. They were out of this world. We were going to make some big bucks!

After we baked tons of cookies, we all helped Daniel make more origami birds, and then back at our own houses we chose some toys and books we had grown out of to sell. I didn't have many, because I'd given stuff away before we moved, so I took a deep breath and picked a couple of toys that I still played with. It was hard work being charitable sometimes.

I wished I had more things to sell. I couldn't stop thinking about what might happen if the mosque did shut down. Mom and Dad might not find their secret smiles in any other mosque, and we'd all have to travel much farther. Other people from the community wouldn't have a nearby place to pray and meet their friends, either. And Mrs. Rogers wouldn't be able to come to the next Eid celebration at the mosque like she wants to.

It made me feel all worried again, thinking about that, so I sent Allah a quick little prayer.

"Please, please let the talent contest go well."

CHAPTER 13

At breakfast on Monday morning, Maryam said, "Omar, shall I show you where your room is? It looks like you've forgotten, because YOU KEEP COMING INTO MINE!"

I gulped down the spoonful of porridge I had in my mouth and stared at her, wondering what the big problem was.

"What are you staring at? Seriously. You came in the other day when I was with my friends, and you even came in last night when I was sleeping, fumbling about like an **aMoeba brain!**"

"What? Why would I—"

"I bet you were looking for things to sell at your stupid talent show."

"Maryam!" Mom stepped in. "That's quite enough rudeness from you. How dare you accuse Omar of swiping things from your room."

"What? I don't believe it. You always take his side. **HE'S THE ONE COMING INTO MY ROOM!**"

Maryam gave up on her breakfast and folded her arms.

Dad said, "It's quite all right for Omar to come into your room, you know. We don't treat family like strangers. And, after all, he's your dearest, darlingest, *only* brother—you never know when you might need to depend on each other."

I giggled. And even Maryam giggled and quickly pointed out Dad's mistake. "What about Esa?"

"Oh yeah, I forgot we had him." Dad winked.

Esa turned over his bowl of Coco Pops in protest. That almost made us late. Almost.

There's nothing Mom and Dad hate more

than lateness. So even a

is factored into our

"getting-ready time" in

the mornings. Super nerdy,

I know.

I knew the rest of the day was going to pass

sooooo slowly, because I absolutely couldn't

wait for talent contest day. By the time I got into

bed that evening, I felt like I'd lived through a

million hours, not just fourteen.

o o o

On Tuesday morning, as I was hopping into the

Peanut, my heart was racing. Talent contest

day—

OH YEAAAH!

Mrs. Rogers was in her driveway, putting her trash out. "Omar, is your spa open today? I could do with a foot rub."

"Not today, Mrs. Rogers, but you can come to the talent contest," I shouted through the car window.

And then I thought about the fact that I hadn't ever seen her feet . . . What if they were covered in **fungus** and she had really long toenails because she's too old to bend over and cut them?

EWWWWW!

I was SUPER NERVOUS all day.
Was it going to go well? Was it going to be a
big hit? What if nobody turned up to watch?
What if we didn't sell any cookies?

Charlie checked and double-checked and
triple-checked that we had everything ready
and in place for the evening. Charlie and
Daniel practiced their talents, and basically so
did the whole rest of the playground.

The *Green Eggs and Ham* kid had added
cartwheels to his act, and I could have sworn
Sarah was humming through all of math and
social studies.

When I went into the bathroom, I practiced
smiling in the mirror, but it made me feel silly,
so I stopped. I wasn't entering the contest
anyway, so I didn't really need to worry about

whether a smile-hypnosis act would work. I

focused on how busy I'd be with the judging, to

help calm my nerves.

In the evening, Mom took me back to school

early to meet my friends and set everything up.

The rest of the family, including Mrs. Rogers,

was going to turn up with all the other guests.

I brought my toys to donate and a big box of samosas that Mom had made and said we could sell at 50 cents each. They smelled so **yummy** and were so **CRISPY** that they made my tummy grumble and get confused about whether it was nervous or hungry. I shoved one into my mouth as we walked toward the auditorium.

When we got through the door, I spotted Mrs. Hutchinson right away. She was talking to someone really tall who I'd never seen before. I walked over, and that's the first time I met him . . .

LANCELOT MACINTOSH.

"Ah, hello, Omar," Mrs. Hutchinson said. She turned to the man she was talking to and said, "This is the young boy I was telling you about."

The man gave a little flourishy bow and said to me, "Lancelot Macintosh at your service! I'm the uncle. Your teacher's uncle, that is. And luckily, a school board member, too, so I have the honor of helping to judge

the contest with you this evening." And he
smiled a real smile, the kind that makes
your eyes smile, too. I wondered if he had an
actual hypnosis smile, because I liked him
right away! I liked his WeiRd MuStAcHe —
it was the kind you only see on French
waiters in cartoons, all curled up at the sides.
Nobody *real* has that kind of mustache. But
Lancelot Macintosh did. He smelled of

bubble gum

and he was holding a fancy walking stick that
he didn't seem to need at all. He was wearing a
tweed jacket and pants that were too short for
him, with bright-red socks peeking out from
underneath. I wondered if it was because he was
so tall he couldn't find any to fit. And then he said,

"Yeessss. Marvelous. Marvelous,"

for no apparent reason.

A third-grade teacher walked past in a hurry, sending her light-as-a-feather silk scarf gliding down to the floor, but Lancelot Macintosh spun around and caught it on his walking stick before it hit the ground. He wasn't even looking in her direction when it fell! SO cool! He plucked it off the stick and gave it to me.

He smiled. "Why don't you return that to its owner?"

I did, and the teacher was so happy, she put $5 in my donation box.

I went right back to Lancelot Macintosh, though, because he was so interesting. Daniel and Charlie had arrived, and Lancelot Macintosh was telling them about a man who had been the Formula One world champion THREE times even though he was involved in a big accident. He'd just started answering the MiLLiON QUESTiONS we had about it when Mrs. Hutchinson reminded us we had a big job to do. We all scurried off to finish setting up the chairs and putting up a banner on the stage—in just half an hour, the show would be starting!

CHAPTER 14

The show went off with a *BANG.*

I mean, *really* it did, because one kid from sixth grade thought it would be cool to do a science experiment onstage, and he must have put too much of something in, because it made a big scary noise and there was yucky stuff everywhere.

I sneaked a quick look at Mom and Dad, who had their proud and disappointed faces on at the same time. They were probably so excited about someone else loving science enough to do it as their talent and disappointed that he'd messed it up.

We saw handstands, ballet, singing, more singing, poetry, tae kwon do, acting, more singing, break dancing, juggling and,

Oh, for the love of pancakes,

more singing!

Lancelot Macintosh clapped really loud for each kid and said, *"Marvelous!"* as if their talent was the best thing he had ever seen. Except for when the science went wrong, which is when he said, *"Ah, toads!"*

Sometimes his reactions were more fun to watch than the performers themselves. I couldn't stop glancing at him. Every so often, he would twiddle his mustache, and twice he looked over at me and winked.

Then it was intermission, which is when people could walk around and buy the stuff we were selling. Everyone was talking about the cookies. They were the first to sell out, and the samosas were next. Daniel's origami birds weren't doing so badly, either. Lancelot Macintosh bought five. And he never leaned on his walking stick. Not once. I wondered why he even had it. It was like a prop. Maybe for tap dancing? I thought he was probably full of mysterious surprises.

By the way, you might be wondering why I keep calling Lancelot Macintosh by his full name. That's because he is one of those people whose name *has* to be said in full. You can't just call him Lancelot or Mr. Macintosh. It doesn't sound right at all.

The performances after intermission were more exciting. The *Green Eggs and Ham* kid came on. Somebody had cleverly attached a microphone to his sweater, so we could still hear him when he was upside down. I heard Mrs. Hutchinson whispering happily along with some of the words.

Daniel and Charlie had decided to do an act together in the end, because Charlie had felt a bit too shy to do one on his own. Daniel sang

a song by an old band called the Beatles while

Charlie did an awesome

ROBOT DANCE

that made the most of his

weird double-jointed

elbows. They

looked like

they were

having the most fun ever,

even more than the time they

had a competition to see who

could fit the most Whoppers

into their mouth!

Then a girl from fourth grade came on

wearing a Batman costume and did the best

Batman impression I've ever seen
a kid do, because kids have

SQUEAK

voices and Batman does not. But that wasn't
all! She had on a Spider-Man costume
underneath, and she hung from the curtain as
if she had sticky spider fingers. Then she had
an Iron Man costume under that! I couldn't
believe all the voices she could do.

Lancelot Macintosh loved this. He stood up
and said,

"Bravo!"

That was the final performance, so we had a mini break while the judges wrote down their choices. I chose the last girl as the winner, and the *Green Eggs and Ham* kid as the runner-up.

Mrs. Hutchinson gathered together our slips of paper, and her curls seemed to get

EXTRA BOUNCY

as she read them all. "We picked exactly the same winner and runner-up—it's unanimous!"

Then she went onto the stage to announce the results, but first she said, "We wouldn't be here today if it weren't for a young man who hasn't performed but who has a great talent of his own. Omar has shown love, compassion and drive. He cares greatly about how it would affect others if our local mosque were to close down—and he did something about it! That, to me, is just as much of a talent as doing something onstage, Omar. We are proud of you, and of Charlie and Daniel.

Well done."

For a minute, I thought I felt a lump in my throat. Nah, it must just have been the samosa I had shoved in earlier . . .

CHAPTER 15

After the show, when everybody had left,

Mrs. Hutchinson counted up the cash. Then

Mr. Martin, the custodian, started cleaning up

all the mess. There were a LOT of napkins and

cookie crumbs on the floor. Dad said we should

all give Mr. Martin a hand by

putting the chairs away,

so we did.

Then Mrs. Hutchinson and Mr. McLeary came over to Mom and me, saying it was important to give me the cash right away. Lancelot Macintosh referred to it as "the day's takings."

There was
$1,419.50.

My shoulders

dropped.

"Oh . . ." I said. "That sounds like a long way off from $30,000."

We'd worked so hard, for so long. Maybe making money wasn't as easy as I'd always thought it was.

"A marvelous amount, young boy!" said Lancelot Macintosh.

"You've done so well, Omar," Dad chipped in. "You don't realize it, but that's a whole lot of money, and it's going to go a long way toward helping the mosque."

"But it won't save it," I said.

"Don't worry," said Mom. "Lots of other people are raising money, too. I'm sure it will all add up to the amount they need."

I looked at Maryam, remembering that she and her friends were trying, too.

Mrs. Hutchinson's curls looked sad for me. I didn't want them to be sad, so I gave my best smile and said, "It's great! Thank you for your help, Mrs. Hutchinson and Mr. McLeary. I'm going to keep thinking and come up with more ideas!"

I shoved the envelope of cash into Mom's bag, and everyone got back to putting the chairs away. When I glanced up, Lancelot Macintosh was staring into space and twiddling his mustache as if he was thinking about something very deeply. Funny. I wondered what was on his mind.

Mom and Dad could not stop talking about how proud they were of me on the way home.

Mrs. Rogers said I was the

best could-be grandson she ever had.

Maryam said nothing, but she did grunt every time someone else said something nice. I thought it would be kind to give Maryam some of the spotlight. After all, she had been working hard to sell her art for the mosque, too. Also, I was curious to know if she was making enough to save the mosque. So I said, "How's your art stuff going, Maryam?"

Maryam looked a bit like Esa does when he's been caught drawing with Mom's lipstick. "G-great. Really great, actually! I sold three pieces for $500 each."

"Wow, that's amazing," I said.

But Dad said, "*Did* you, now?" In his I'm-your-dad-and-I-know-when-you're-lying voice.

"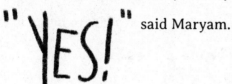" said Maryam.

"I DID!"

And then when Mom gave her an it's-OK-dear look, as we pulled into our drive, she practically

BURST iNTO FLAMES.

She flung the car door open and jumped out, saying, "Don't believe me, then—you never do!"

We all gave each other the look we do when Maryam acts like a complete teenager. Dad followed her to her room to talk to her, and the rest of us fell into our beds, exhausted.

Before I fell asleep, I thought about the cash in Mom's purse. I imagined it

multiplying like bacteria

to get to $30,000. Yup, Mom and Dad even love making us learn the yucky science stuff! Bacteria can go from being just one of them to hundreds of them in minutes. Imagine if money could do that, too . . . But I bet if it did, Maryam would try to steal it because she'd be so jealous.

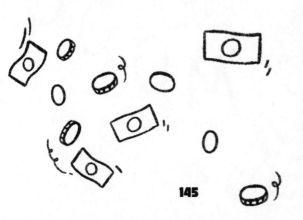

CHAPTER 16

When I woke up the next morning to get ready for school, I thought I'd take a quick peek at the cash. Maybe Allah had performed a miracle and it *actually* had multiplied!

I went to get Mom's bag. But when I opened it, the envelope wasn't there.

"MOOOO

OOOOM!

I yelled.

"Did you put the money somewhere else?"

"No," said Mom. "What is going on? Isn't it in there?"

"No. It's not.

Wheeeerrrrre issssssssss ittttttttt?"

I was super panicked.

Dad came back into the house with his motorcycle helmet on. He looked like an

AL!EN DAD.

"What's happening?"

"The money is gone!" I said.

"Such melodrama," said Maryam, who was eating her breakfast already.

"I want pancakes," said Esa.

Dad took off his helmet, as if he needed to scratch his head to think. "Right. Maybe it dropped out at school? Or you didn't put it in the bag?"

"I did. I did." I scratched my head, too.

"Are you 100% certain?"

"Yes. Super certain.

500%
certain!"

"Oh Allah," said Mom.

Dad turned to her and said, "I'll go with Omar to the school and find out what's going on." Then to me, he said, "Go and get your helmet." Now I was thrilled and worried at the same time. I hardly EVER get to ride on Dad's bike with him. It felt

like I was in a movie, and Dad and I were the

HEROES

whizzing around to save the day. Hopefully . . .

We raced into school, and Dad explained the whole situation to the school secretary. I tried to stand patiently while he did that, but I was feeling very *im*patient. Finally, the secretary got everyone together. Mrs. Hutchinson, Mr. McLeary, Dad and I all searched the auditorium super thoroughly. I was kind of sure the envelope would be found behind the curtains or inside one of the stacks of chairs, but when it wasn't, I started having trouble breathing.

"Let's check the hallways that lead to the parking lot," said Mr. McLeary.

So there was still hope.

Nothing was there, though. I felt really panicky. Where was it? How could it have just

vanished?

There was still the parking lot. But because that was the last place to check, I was absolutely frantic and was finding it harder and harder to concentrate on searching.

It wasn't there, either.

It was nowhere to be found.

At that point, Mrs. Hutchinson confirmed that she had seen me putting it in Mom's bag.

The conclusion?

The money had been

STOLEN.

Everyone was really worried. Mrs. Hutchinson's hair was doing things I'd never seen it do before.

I was trying to be brave. I held on to my hero-in-the-movies helmet. The hero wouldn't cry. I wouldn't, either. I wouldn't. But then Dad took me into a hug, with all his leather motorcycle gear and his strong arms and his dad smell, and I cried.

I cried a lot.

CHAPTER 17

Charlie and Daniel were super upset when I told them about the money.

Daniel kicked a tree stump and then fell on the ground, yelling out in pain.

"The tree didn't take the money!" I said.

"But someone did," said Charlie. "We can't let them get away with it."

"Yeah!" said Daniel.

"Let's make a list of **SUSPECTS!**" said Charlie, excited. "I mean, nobody knows the details better than we do."

I perked up.

I loved this idea!

I got us started. "OK. Who was around at the end, when Mrs. Hutchinson gave me the money?"

"Us. Your parents. My parents," said Charlie. "Daniel's parents. Mr. Martin. Mrs. Hutchinson, Mr. McLeary, Lancelot Macintosh, Mrs. Rogers, and Maryam."

Then we all started talking at once about who we thought did it.

We had a pretty good list of suspects and their possible reasons for doing it.

1. MARYAM

Has been jealous right from the start. Big meanie. Super sneaky and quiet, so could easily have taken it.

MOTIVE: Wants to use the money to pretend she's sold some of her art, which she hasn't, and to destroy Omar's plans.

2. MR. MARTIN

Was heard grumbling about cleaning the place up when he thought nobody was near him. Something about "not getting

paid enough for this nonsense." Had a good chance to snatch the money because nobody was paying attention to him as he cleaned.

MOTIVE: Disgruntled about not getting paid enough. Needs the money.

3. LANCELOT MACINTOSH

Nobody is that nice and cheery. In the movies, it's always the nice guy, the one everyone likes, so it must be him.

MOTIVE: Needs money to replace the clothes in his closet, because they all shrank in the wash (which is why his pants are so short).

4. MR. McSCARY

Maybe he really *is* scary and was just pretending to be nice so he could spoil everything. He's the principal, so he could stand near Mom's

bag without anyone thinking he was up to something.

MOTIVE: Wants to make us pay. For what? Ummmmmm, for being kids. He hates kids.

We completely ruled out Mrs. Hutchinson and any of our parents. We debated about Mrs. Rogers. I know her the most and I was super definitely 500% sure that it wasn't her, but Daniel and Charlie insisted she'd had the best chance to take the cash while she was in the car with us. I didn't like it, but I added her to the list.

5. MRS. ROGERS

Always full of surprises and often has a sly smile on her face. Had a good chance to snatch the money in the car.

MOTIVE: Just for some entertainment, because she's funny like that.

And just for the fun of it, and to make us feel a bit better, we imagined some out-of-this-world suspects, too.

6. MIND MONSTER

Stormed in and simply took the money right before our very eyes, but he controlled our minds so that we didn't realize what was

happening until the next day, when he was already halfway back to Zeyr, the planet he came from.

MOTIVE: The ruler of Zeyr needs the money to plant trees, which they don't have on their planet.

7. INVISIBLE MAN

Strolled in, dipped his hand in Mom's bag and

took the money without anyone seeing him. MOTIVE: Chooses to use his invisibility for evil, rather than good. (Which, by the way, is the opposite of what I would do if I was invisible. I'd go and shut down factories that make too much pollution by flicking off their switches and leaving everyone wondering what happened.)

We decided to carefully investigate each of our suspects over the next few days.

"You live by Mrs. Rogers and with Maryam, so you'll have to cover them," Daniel said to me.

"Uh-huh," I said, feeling a bit sick in my tummy.

"Don't worry," Charlie said. "Daniel and

I will work on Mr. Martin and Mr. McScary, and we can figure out how to get to Lancelot Macintosh together."

"Thanks, guys," I said, slumping my shoulders.

o o o

That whole evening, Maryam was super annoying. She watched her

boring TV shows

instead of agreeing to play *Minecraft* with me. I kept wondering if she did it or not: Would she really spoil things like that?

Over dinner, as I pushed my food around my plate because my tummy felt like it wasn't going to accept any food at all—like it was going to chuck anything I swallowed right back up and out of the mouth I dared to chew with—I said to Maryam, "What do you think should happen to the person who stole the mosque money?"

Dad raised an eyebrow.

Maryam shrugged. "I don't know. Go to prison probably. Right, Dad?"

Hmmmmm, quite a normal response. It was so hard to figure out if she did it.

Dad said, "I hope whoever it was gets caught, and if they do, the authorities will deal with them."

Esa starting throwing his peas off his plate one by one.

"What on earth are you doing, Esa?" said Mom, jumping up.

"I can't eat those," he said.

"They're not halal."

We all exploded with laughter. Maryam sprayed juice all over herself and the table.

EWWWWW.

"Fruit and vegetables are always halal, dummy!" said Maryam, cleaning herself off.

As she wiped her mouth, I thought about
Lancelot Macintosh's mustache.

Was it some kind of disguise?

Also, why did he come to our talent contest?
And could he make himself invisible?

CHAPTER 18

The next day, the most exciting thing happened during language arts. Charlie was sent to get some photocopies of our worksheets, and he came back all out of breath and wide-eyed with what looked like both

FEAR and EXCITEMENT.

(It was sort of like the time he ate too much strawberry licorice and went all hyperactive.)

He sat down and said, "I can't believe I'm still alive.

AAARRGH!

It was so fun but so terrifying."

"What was? What did you do?" I whispered.

"Tell us," said Daniel.

Charlie stood up and then sat down again and then tried to find his pencil before he finally blurted out,

"I broke into Mr. McScary's office."

"You? BROKE? You broke into . . . ?" I managed.

"Whoooooa. Yes, Charlie!" said Daniel.

"OK, well, actually I didn't have to break in—the door was open. But I went in!!! I could see from the photocopy room that he wasn't

there, and I really didn't know when he might come back, but something in me just said, DO IT, and my legs started running without my brain giving permission!"

"What did you find?" I asked, still in shock.

"I was looking for the stolen money, but it wasn't there."

"That doesn't mean that he didn't do it, does it? He might have spent it."

"Yes, you're right, but I saw a copy of

a letter on his desk that he had written to

the local police station . . . and, well, it was

all about the missing money and said how

upset he was about the whole thing and how

he wants them to do more to help us. And,

well . . . I *might* have taken the letter, and

it possibly . . . *might* be in my pocket."

Charlie breathed quickly in and out and

bounced on his chair.

"Never in a MILLION YEARS

would I have imagined you doing that, Charlie!

I'm rubbing off on you!" Daniel gave him a

proud slap on the back.

"Show us," I squealed.

Charlie handed over the letter, and we

passed it to each other secretly, ignoring nosy

glances from Ellie and Sarah.

"Yup. He's innocent," I said.

"Innocent," agreed Daniel.

"I feel like a SECRET AGENT or something." Charlie looked at his hands as if he couldn't quite believe what they'd done.

"You are, Charlie! That's one suspect down, four to go. We're like SUPER SPIES." My brain went into overdrive, trying to think of how we were going to investigate everyone else. How could three kids be more like James Bond?

Daniel had his thinking face on. "I think I have a plan for Mr. Martin . . ."

Charlie and I leaned in just as Mrs. Hutchinson noticed that we weren't really concentrating on our worksheets.

"Boys, don't make me come over there to find out what you're chatting about," she said in her voice that she uses to mean I'm not mad, but I will be in approximately 47 seconds.

Super spying was going to have to wait.

o o o

At home that evening, I couldn't decide whether to think of moneymaking ideas or spying ideas—it made my head hurt! To cheer myself up, I imagined H_2O trying to be a super spy and hiding his huge dragon body behind a tree, which made me laugh out loud.

The deadline for the mosque building work was drawing closer and closer. We only had eight days left. I looked through my keepsake box for inspiration and found a painting Esa had given me when he was two years old. It was in quite good condition and was of birds made out of his handprints in bright colors. I had kept it because it was so cute (don't tell anyone just how much I love him, OK?). I figured if it meant something to me, it might mean a lot to Dad.

So I went to look for Dad, and found him in the garden, pulling out some weeds, probably in exchange for Mom cooking dinner tonight.

Dad would never do gardening just because he wanted to.

"Dad, will you buy this for $5,000?" I showed him the card. "Esa will never have tiny hands like this ever again . . ."

Just then, Mrs. Rogers popped her head over the hedge and said, "How's the moneymaking going?"

"That depends," I answered. "Dad? Was that a yes?"

"Um, no." Dad shook his head.

"It's going badly, Mrs. Rogers," I said.

But I laughed. I guess that had been a pretty

RiDiCULOUS

way to try to make some quick money. Dad and

Mrs. Rogers laughed, too.

"You keep the painting, Omar—Esa made it especially for you. But I'll let you have $10 for helping me with the weeds," said Dad, opening his wallet.

"Cool!" I said, and stuck the money in my jeans pocket.

"And we could make some more cookies for you to sell, Omar," Mrs. Rogers added kindly. "I know they won't raise as much as the talent show, but every little bit helps, eh?"

Then and there, I decided to cross Mrs.

Rogers off our suspect list. There was just

NO WAY she'd taken the

money—she'd helped us a ton, and she'd been

really looking forward to visiting the mosque

with us, too.

Nope,
she definitely
didn't
deserve to be
on there.

CHAPTER 19

The next person we investigated was Mr.

Martin, following Daniel's super - spy plan.

Daniel had decided we should watch the

custodian during lunchtime so that we could

set a THIEF TRAP. We had started the

day we made our suspect list, and soon learned

that his routine went like clockwork. The

important part for our plan was that every day

at 1:20 he went to the old shed on the edge of

our playground to return the broom and mop

he'd used in the morning.

On Friday, we were ready to put our plan

into action. I felt really nervous—the mosque's

deadline was coming up,

and we still had no idea

whether we would find

the culprit.

At 1:15, Daniel quickly

ran over to the shed while

Charlie and I kept watch. He left his Batman

wallet just outside the shed door so Mr. Martin

couldn't miss it. It had $5 in it, too. Daniel

knew this was a big risk, because he might not

get his money back, but he said he was happy

to do it if we could find the thief.

Daniel ran back to us with his eyes all

BIG LIKE SAUCERS and we

all went to sit next to the tree that would give

us the best view of the shed without looking

suspicious.

"So," Charlie said, "if he keeps the wallet,

he's dishonest and he's probably the one who

did it."

"Exactly," said Daniel, rubbing his hands together and licking his lips. He was really getting into this spying job!

Just a couple of minutes later, Mr. Martin appeared. For a second, we thought he hadn't seen the wallet and we all held our breath while we waited to see what he'd do. Was our plan ruined? But after he put the broom and the mop away, he picked it up and looked around in a  Shifty way,  like he was searching for who could have dropped it and whether they'd seen him find it.

THE PLAN HAD WORKED!

We all made big eyes at each other.

But that afternoon in math, there was a knock on the door, and Mr. Martin came in looking worried. He'd been going around to all the classes to ask if anyone had lost their wallet.

Daniel made a big show of being really relieved to have it back and said *thank you* about ten times. For a second, my tummy felt like it was scrunching itself up into a marble-size ball, but Charlie squeezed my hand and whispered,

"Innocent."

He was right. Maybe the trick had been worth it, because now Mr. Martin was officially off the suspect list. It didn't

really make my tummy feel better, though,

and all this ruling out of people made me

EXTRA NERV😟US

because it made it more likely that it could be

Maryam. It did seem like she had a very strong

reason for doing it . . . I kept thinking of her

objective: Make more money than
Omar and his friends.

I had to find out once and for all, so when

Maryam went to take a shower that evening,

I crept into her room. If she had done it,

the money would still be there, because

she wouldn't have been able to spend it or

donate it to the mosque fund without causing

suspicion.

I started with her dresser, slowly sliding

each drawer open, hoping not to see a bunch of cash, and just then:

"OMMMMMMAAA

It was Maryam. She had come back to get her special girly shower gel that she keeps in her bedroom so no one uses it by accident.

"How dare you? This is the last straw! You're such an annoying brat and I'm telling Dad!" she threatened.

Then I did something that Maryam hadn't expected me to do. And I hadn't really expected to do. I threw myself into her big sister arms and cried.

"I'm sorry," I sobbed through snot and tears.

AARRRRR!"

"I just had to see if you took it, because I'm desperate and I'm sad and I'm worried and my tummy won't stop hurting."

Maryam hugged me back and told me to sit down. "I would never do that to you, Omar . . . Yes, I do call you names and tease you and things. And YES, you get on my nerves ALL THE TIME...

but still, you're my *only* brother."

That made us both laugh.

183

"Seriously," she said. "I would never actually do anything that made you or Esa sad for real. I promise."

I believed her. Because her hug felt real and not even Maryam can lie that well. I gave her one more hug and crossed her off our list.

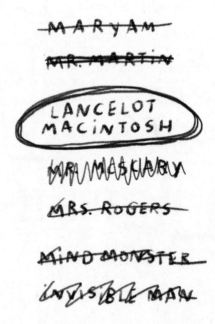

CHAPTER 20

The countdown to the mosque's deadline felt

like it was going faster and faster and faster

the closer we got to it. We had managed to

talk to all of our suspects except Lancelot

Macintosh. But with just two days to go, and

since we'd ruled everyone else out, we decided

that he had to be the

**PRIME
SUSPECT.**

"Should we tell the police?" said Charlie at lunchtime.

"They won't listen to a bunch of kids," said Daniel.

"We have to try to lure him back into school," I thought out loud. "Maybe if we tell Mrs. Hutchinson we really liked him and we want him to visit our class, she'd ask him?"

"We did like him!" said Daniel and Charlie, freakishly at the same time.

"I know . . . I wish it wasn't him . . ." We liked him a lot. But maybe that's why we should be suspicious of him, we decided. In movies, it's NEVER the person you expect.

We took our request to Mrs. Hutchinson, who thought it would be a wonderful idea. But she said that Lancelot Macintosh was an extremely busy man, so we'd probably have to wait at least a couple of weeks!

Even though we weren't going to be able to cross him off our list until it was too late to save the mosque, we couldn't stop talking about him, and all the things that were unusual and might make him a suspicious character:

"He smells like bubble gum when he's never even chewing any. What is that about?"

"He holds a walking stick he doesn't use!"

"He really is too cheery."

"He uses words that nobody else does. Ever."

"His pants are too short for him."

○ ○ ○

I was super disappointed when Saturday
morning rolled around. That meant zero days
left to the deadline. Mom and Dad had said
that before the prayer, the imam was going to
talk about how much money we had all raised.

But the police hadn't found the missing
money.

We hadn't talked to our prime suspect.

And I didn't think Maryam had sold any art.

There was no doubt about it:

the secret-smile mosque was going to shut down.

I was certain this would be the last time we went there. They were going to have to do a big goodbye because I hadn't been able to save it. I couldn't breathe. The air wasn't going into my lungs. I felt like I had suddenly been dropped onto another planet where breathing wasn't even a thing. I grabbed my neck in a panic.

I imagined H_2O blowing his cool steam toward my face. That made me breathe better. But I had to imagine him flying alongside the Peanut all the way to the mosque.

We took our shoes off and went in. There was **pin-drop silence**. I guess that's how it's supposed to be in the mosque, but there's always some aunty gossiping with another aunty, or some panicky dad calling out his child's name because he can't see her hiding behind one of the pillars.

We sat on the soft carpet and watched gloomily as the imam walked in.

But his shoulders weren't slumping and his lips weren't turned down. They were curled up into a surprising smile. And his chest was out, as if he was proud.

WHAAAAAT?

Why would he be happy that the mosque had to close down?

Then he said, "Dear brothers and sisters, children, neighbors and friends, I am so pleased to announce that we have *raised all the money* we needed to save the mosque. There have been many generous donations from all of you, and even young children have been going out in their communities to fundraise. Together we raised an amazing $25,000. But we still didn't think we would make it until we had an unexpected donation last week of a whopping $5,000 from a complete stranger—a Mr. Lancelot Macintosh."

WHAAAAAT?

I practically choked on my own saliva. I couldn't believe it. What? Whaaaaat? Lancelot

Macintosh? Our prime suspect? What the Batman bananas was this? Where did he get $5,000? He couldn't even buy himself pants that fit, so how could he give money to the mosque? Nothing made sense.

CHAPTER 21

Mom and Dad were as flabbergasted as I was. They didn't have the answers to my questions, either. But one thing was for sure: their secret smiles were as sparkly as ever.

In fact, I had never seen so many teeth on display at the mosque before. Yellow ones, white ones, missing ones, crooked ones, perfect ones, braced ones and even gold ones. All in the most

GINORMOUS

Smiles.

I couldn't WAIT to get to school and ask Mrs. Hutchinson what was going on.

When we got home, I found a shiny quarter on the driveway, which I decided was an extra piece of luck. I snatched it up quickly before Maryam saw it, and shoved it into my jeans. That's when I felt the $10 bill Dad had given me for weeding. I had completely forgotten to donate it at the mosque, so I shot upstairs to my secret underwear hiding place to keep it safe.

I put my hand into the back of the closet to fish out my green underwear, but something was different.

"WHAT THE BUS ?!!"

The envelope of cash from the talent contest was there! With all the money. Every bit of it.

OHHHHHH MyyYyyy GOSHHH!

I screamed all the way back down the stairs, tripped over my own foot and crawl-hopped through the hallway into the kitchen, where everyone was.

"I found the money!"

Mom and Dad looked extremely confused.

"It was in my secret hiding place!"

"Wow. That's. Wow. Alhamdulilah," said Mom, which basically means "thank Allah."

"Who else knows about the hiding place?" asked Dad, scratching his head again.

"Nobody. Just me."

"That's a mystery . . ." said Dad. "So weird."

"Wait!" shouted Maryam, and she darted up the stairs at the speed of light.

"What's gotten into her now?" said Mom.

Maryam came back with her phone in her hand. "Look, look. This explains *everything*."

She unlocked her phone and brought up a video on the screen. It was a video of me. Or was it a *zombie?* Well, at least I looked as if I was the star of some sort of zombie show. I didn't have blood all over my face or anything, but I was definitely different than usual. Maryam was saying things to me, but I was just walking around like I couldn't hear her.

"I recorded this after the talent show, when Omar came into my room AGAIN. But I was so sleepy I forgot all about it, and I only just remembered," said Maryam. "Now look carefully at his hand. He's holding a white envelope!"

We all looked up from the phone at each other's faces.

"He sleepwalks!"

declared Maryam. "He moved the money when he was sleepwalking!"

Dad laughed. "Wow. And this whole time, we were going nuts thinking someone had stolen it."

I opened my mouth wide like a shocked emoji.

"Why do you think you hid it, Omar?" asked Maryam.

"Well, I was thinking about the money before I slept and that you'd be really jealous about it . . ."

For that, I got a whack on the arm from Maryam, and Maryam got an eyeballing from Dad. Then Maryam got a pinch on the arm from me, and I got an eyeballing from Dad.

Then Esa said,

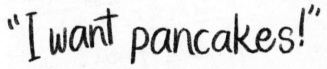

"I want pancakes!"

and Mom decided it was time for lunch.

By the time food was on the table, we'd stopped being shocked and found it hilarious instead. I couldn't wait to tell Charlie and Daniel, and give the money to the mosque. We giggled about it for the rest of the day.

Poor Lancelot Macintosh, I thought. *He never should have been a suspect at all.* And it turned out THE MOST SUPER OF SUPER SPIES WAS *Maryam,* not me or Daniel or Charlie! I guess she's not such a bad big sister after all . . .

CHAPTER 22

I practically flew into school on Monday

morning, and when I skidded into the classroom,

I saw him sitting there on Mrs. Hutchinson's

chair. Walking stick in hand. Pants too short.

Lancelot MacIntosh!

I pounced on him with the biggest hug ever

and didn't let go until Mrs.

Hutchinson started asking

why I was

stuck to her

uncle like a

baby koala

Lancelot Macintosh had come in to talk to the class, just like we'd asked him to when he was our prime suspect.

And you won't believe this: we found out that Lancelot Macintosh is super rich. He's practically a

GaZILLiONaiRe.

When he was a "young lad" he had invented a small *thiNGaMaJiG* that has gone into all cars ever built since then.

He told us all about it, saying "Marvelous, marvelous" every other sentence and twiddling his mustache at least twenty times.

"So what do you do now, Mr. Lancelot

Macintosh?" asked Sarah. "Do you just sit around and count your money?"

Lancelot Macintosh laughed a real hearty laugh. "Well, I keep myself very busy trying to invent new things. Some serious things and some things just for the fun of it!"

Yup, it turns out that Lancelot Macintosh spends a lot of time trying to invent new flavors of bubble gum in his house. That explains a lot!

When he was leaving, he said quietly to me, "Omar, you remind me of myself when I was a young chap. You really impressed me with your marvelous attitude. It reminded me of the days when I chased my dreams and

DIDN'T GIVE UP ON A THING."

"Thanks! Is that why you gave the money to the mosque?" I asked.

"Yes, because I want you to believe in yourself and never forget the community that will be there to support you while you're chasing your dreams."

I beamed.

Then he chuckled and said, "Either that or something about that big smile of yours must have made me do it."

No way, I thought. *I guess it works after all:*

my hypnosis smile!

Charlie and Daniel threw me their *OHHHH WOWWWW* looks.

o o o

At home, when I filled Mom and Dad in about Lancelot Macintosh, they were really impressed. Dad was even familiar with the *thingamajig* that he invented and couldn't believe he had met someone who had contributed to his driving experience so much.

Even Maryam was in a good mood, talking about how she loved his mustache style. "It's so hipster," she said, like she even knows what that means.

Mrs. Rogers was over for a cup of tea, and she said, "I could alter his pants to fit, you know."

"I bet he could pay *The Queen* to alter pants that fit with all that money," Mom said, laughing.

"I think he wears them like that on purpose," I said. "And I like him just the way he is."

o o o

That evening, the doorbell rang. I thought it was another of Mom's online orders, but it was Daniel and Charlie.

"WHAAAAAT?"

I didn't know they were coming!

"*I* invited them, turnip nose," said Maryam. But she said it sweetly somehow, as if she was using the funny insult in an affectionate way.

"Why would you invite them??!" I asked.

"Well, I did sell one piece of art," she said. "To Dad!"

"Soooooo?" I was still super confused.

"And I didn't give the money to the mosque."

"You called us here to tell us that?" said Daniel.

"Okaaay," said Charlie.

"Not exactly . . ." Maryam was enjoying this so much.

"Come on, Maryam, stop being weird!" I pleaded.

She giggled. "Follow me, then!"

We all ran up the stairs behind her. In her room, she had three wrapped presents on her bed.

"For you three," she said, pointing.

We jumped on them like they were going to vanish if we didn't open them in three seconds.

WHOA! WHOA! WHOA!

Maryam had bought us the

NERF LASER BLASTERS

that we wanted with the money she had raised.

"Well, you do have panda breath,

but I'm kind of

proud of you," she said.

I pounced on her with a big

hug. Then Charlie joined us, and Daniel

got super excited and jumped on us, too.

CHAPTER 23

I don't know why, but whenever something unusual happens in my life, we seem to end up with biryani on our dinner table. Mom and Dad had invited Lancelot Macintosh over for dinner to thank him for what he did for the mosque. Mrs. Hutchinson was coming, too, since he was her uncle and she'd helped so much with the talent show.

That day, Mom and Dad fussed around in the kitchen more than usual and cleaned until their backs hurt, because a gazillionaire had never been to our home before and they were nervous.

"What are you making, Mommy?" asked Esa.

"We're making biryani, spinach curry, naan, samosas, lassi and moussaka."

"Mufasa? From *The Lion King*?" said Esa.

Mom giggled and explained that moussaka was an Arabic dish made with eggplant and ground meat, and not Simba's dad from *The Lion King*.

"Remember when Esa used to call rice 'mice'?" said Maryam, and then, doing a squeaky impression of him, she said, "I want curry and mice for dinner."

While we were in the middle of practically wetting ourselves with laughter, I heard the roar of an engine and I ran to look out the window. There was a bright-yellow Ferrari!

Oh Nutella in a Cake Pop!

For a minute, I thought Allah had finally sent my reward for the fast I kept during Ramadan. But then I saw Lancelot Macintosh and Mrs. Hutchinson hop out.

He is too cool !!!

I guess gazillionaires have lots of money, and people with lots of money can buy expensive nice cars. And it was just like him to go for the most fun color of all.

What happened next was better than anything in the

ENTIRE *universe.*

Can you guess? I got to go for a ride with him before we had dinner! Sure, he didn't let me drive it, even though I offered to pay him the $10 from my secret money-hiding place, but still it was the

Best TIME Ever!

ZANIB MIAN

grew up in London and still lives there today. She was a science teacher for a few years after leaving university, but right from when she was a little girl, her passion was writing stories and poetry. She has released lots of picture books with the independent publisher Sweet Apple Publishers, but the Planet Omar series is the first time she's written for older readers.

NASAYA MAFARIDIK

is based in Indonesia. Self-taught, she has a passion for books and bright, colorful stationery.